E
C.1

Lobel, Arnold
    The turnaround wind.   Harper &
Row, 1988.
    32 p.   col. illus.

I. Title.

THE TURNAROUND WIND

ARNOLD LOBEL

Harper & Row, Publishers

The Turnaround Wind
Copyright © 1988 by the Estate of Arnold Lobel
Printed in the U.S.A. All rights reserved.
10 9 8 7 6 5 4 3 2 1
First Edition

Library of Congress Cataloging-in-Publication Data
Lobel, Arnold.
The turnaround wind.

Summary: The reader turns the book upside down to
see what happens when a fierce wind blows through a
country town one afternoon, affecting many different
people and animals out enjoying the summer air.
[1. Winds—Fiction.]   I. Title.
PZ7.L7795Tu 1988   [E]   87-45293
ISBN 0-06-023987-5
ISBN 0-06-023988-3 (lib. bdg.)

One afternoon in summer, the sky was clear and blue.
The countryside was filled with happy beings.
In every grassy meadow and on every dusty road, they were
walking and talking and taking the air.

There was an organ grinder
and his monkey,

a stout man
and his slender wife,

a nurse wheeling
a crying baby with a bottle,

a maiden
and a soldier,

a thief
looking for things to steal,

a man wearing a turban,

a fisherman
and a watching fish,

the mayor and his wife,

a farmer
with his bull and pig,

and the farmer's wife
with her favorite duck.

There was a little girl
and her faithful dog,

a man reading a book,
a man carrying a cat,

a girl with a red hood
bringing cookies
to her grandmother,

a hunter looking for a fox,

a lady with a cape,
and another with an umbrella.

There was a man
smoking a pipe,
and a lady in a bonnet,

an old sailor and his parrot,

a girl wearing a bow,
a boy with a boat,

and an artist
with a canvas and paints.

Even their royal majesties, the King and Queen,
came out to enjoy the day.

To everyone's astonishment,
dark and ominous clouds
suddenly appeared in the sky.
Down came a strong and rushing wind.
It seemed to turn the whole world
around and around and upside down.

The old sailor's parrot squawked and screeched
as the wind carried her high into the air.
She thought it odd to be flying
without fluttering a single feather.

The organ grinder was confused by the storm.
Although his diamond stickpin stayed firmly in place,
his monkey had completely disappeared.

The slender wife held tightly to her stout husband.
They had been married for forty-five years
and had been through thick and thin together.

The stout man embraced his slender wife because he loved her.
He had no intention of letting her blow away.

In spite of the storm, the nurse did not forget her duty.
"Even in a disaster, baby must have her milk,"
she said as she snatched the baby's bottle out of the air.

The mayor heard a *crunch*.
The baby's bottle left a large jagged hole
in his best top hat.

The baby, who was crying before the storm,
cried even louder.
Its wailing could be heard above the roar of the wind.

The thief wondered
if he could kidnap the baby in the confusion,
but it was crying so loudly that he did not dare.

When the maiden found herself near the soldier,
she smiled broadly, though her teeth
were not as perfect as she would wish.

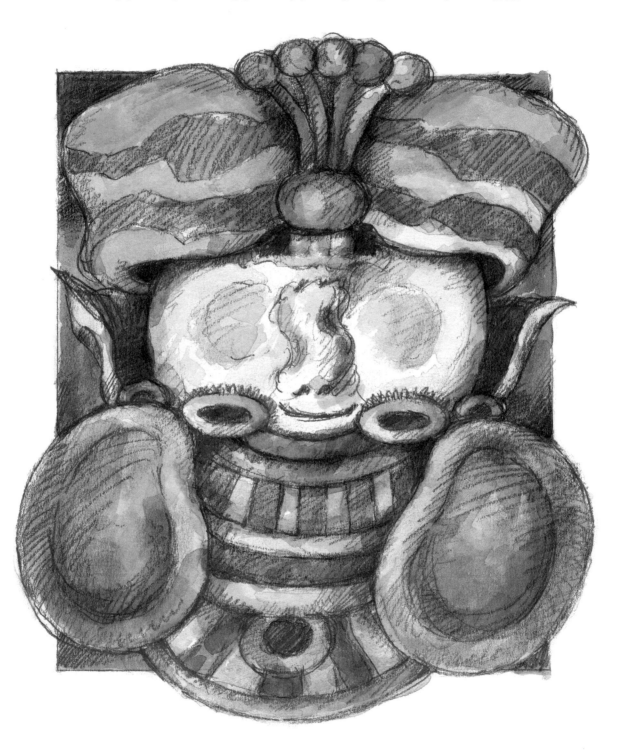

The soldier flashed his dark eyes with delight
because the wind pushed him very close to the maiden.

The mayor's wife thought
that the man wearing the turban was attractive.
When she crashed against him,
she grinned between her rouged cheeks.

The man wearing the turban was displeased
as he abruptly collided with the mayor's wife.

The fisherman lost a grip on his hook and line.
He very nearly caught his own nose as the storm raged.

The bull just bellowed
and put out his tongue to lick the passing wind.

The farmer was shaken by the sudden storm.
He was wide-eyed with wonder and surprise.

The duck promised the farmer's wife
to lay many eggs as soon as the clouds rolled away.

"Oops!" cried the farmer's wife
when the storm splattered her fine duck egg.

The dog, being very faithful to the little girl,
wagged his tongue with joy when he saw that his mistress
was smiling through the storm.

The little girl with the faithful dog
was happy that her pretty cap was staying securely
on her head.

The girl wearing a bow felt it flapping faster and faster.
She looked down and saw that her feet were leaving the ground.
"I do not want to fly!" she cried.

The man reading a book was confused
as all of the pages flipped past his startled eyes.
He was a fast reader, but not that fast.

The cat was terrified.
He heard his master speaking gentle words
of reassurance, but he was not comforted.

The man carrying a cat stood strong against the wind.
"Be calm, my pet," he said.
"The storm will soon be over."

Grandmother was fast.
When she saw the flocks of cookies swooping by her head,
she caught them all in her mouth
and did not miss a single one.

The girl with the red hood was dismayed
as the wind blew the basket out of her hands.
Nearly all of her cookies flew in the air.

The fox, who was as clever as a fox could be,
made sure that the hunter would not find him.
He stayed well hidden behind the moving grass.

The hunter paid no attention to the storm.
He had only one thing on his mind.
He kept his eyes peeled, looking for the fox.

The lady with an umbrella
watched it bend and break in the turbulent air.
She was alarmed and wished that she were safely home in bed.

The lady with a cape was frightened
when she saw it flopping around her in every direction.
She wished that she were safely home with a cup of hot tea.

The pig felt the brisk breezes
tickling the soft places behind his ears.
He giggled gleefully.

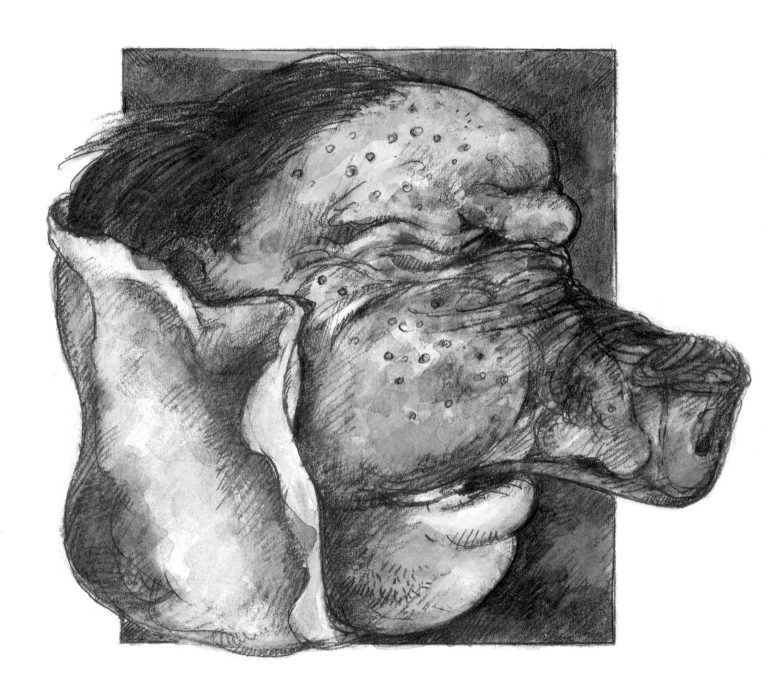

The man with a pipe gasped for breath.
Smoke and ashes billowed into his nose and eyes.

The organ grinder's monkey ate a quick and tasty snack
as he chewed up the bouquet that grew on the lady's bonnet.

The lady with the bonnet felt nervous
as the flowers that decorated it
began to tremble and shake.

The boy with a boat looked in vain for a safe harbor.
Not finding one, he moored his craft against his ear
and waited for the weather to change.

The old sailor saw his beard rippling in the wind.
It reminded him of the large waves in the sea
during great hurricanes of long ago.

By a remarkable accident
they created a charming landscape, suitable for framing.
The artist's paints blew onto his canvas.

The artist was a mess.
His face was splattered
with a rainbow of colorful paints.

The Queen was regal and poised,
but she was not amused by the weather.

The King kept his royal dignity,
but he found the storm most exciting.

Then, as quickly as it began, the storm was over.
The clouds disappeared and the wind stopped.
Everyone dusted themselves off
and walked serenely in the sunshine
of a lovely afternoon.
At sunset they all went home for supper.

All except the thief.
Still looking for things to steal,
he stayed out long, long after dark.